Ihsan and the Wounded Anzac

Written by John Parsons
Illustrated by Pat Reynolds

Contents

Meet the Characters

Ihsan

An old Turkish man.

Ihsan as a young boy.

Zerdali

Ihsan's great-granddaughter.

Bahar

Zerdali's mother, Ihsan's granddaughter.

Old Ekrem

A cafe owner.

An Anzac soldier

A young soldier.

Dear Reader

Many years ago, I visited the Anzac battleground of Gallipoli, in Turkey. It was a silent, sombre place – but to get there, I caught a bus full of happy, spirited Turkish schoolchildren. The contrast made me think about the children who would have lived in the area during more dangerous times.

How might they have reacted to strangers from Australia or New Zealand then?

John Parsons
Author

Krithia and its Surroundings

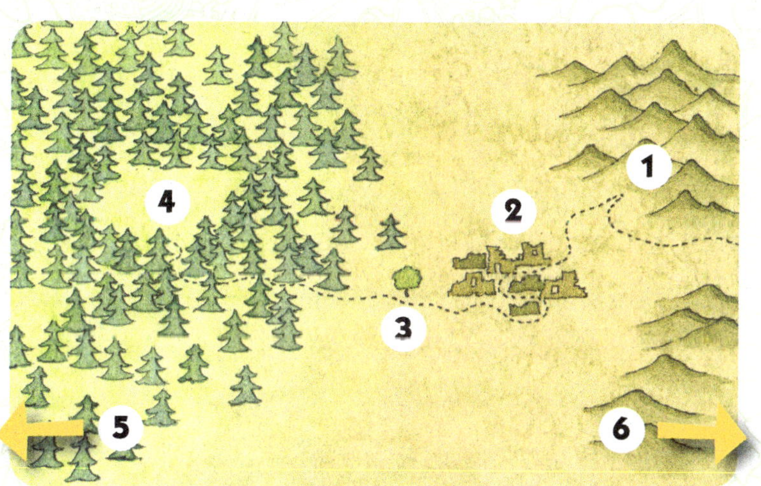

1. The rocky hillside where the goats grazed
2. The town of Krithia
3. The old apricot tree
4. The clearing
5. Anzac cove and the Aegean Sea lie to the west
6. The Bosphorus Strait lies to the east

1 Three Minutes

Zerdali carefully arranged a circle of salty black olives on a small yellow plate and checked her watch. Ten seconds to go.

The moment the second hand swept past the number twelve, she dipped a spoon into the boiling water and expertly scooped out a single egg.

"Not a second longer, not a second too soon," her mother Bahar instructed. "You know your great-grandfather likes his eggs just so."

The perfectly boiled egg slid and jiggled about on the spoon under a stream of cold water from the tap. As soon as the shell was cool enough to touch, Zerdali tapped it against the edge of the sink and carefully peeled the soft-boiled egg.

She laid the egg in the middle of the olives, along with a tiny pinch of salt.

"Salt is not good for Great-Grandfather," Zerdali said to her mother, who was rinsing dried apricots.

"He's almost 97 years old," replied Bahar. "He's been eating boiled eggs and salt since before Turkey even existed as a country. If it's not good for him, he's hiding it well." She picked three of the juiciest apricots and arranged them on the yellow plate.

"There!" she said, smiling at Zerdali. "It's ready."

Zerdali slipped the plate onto a tray and, with a nod to her mother, headed out of the kitchen and into the courtyard. There, shaded by an old spreading olive tree and warmed by a soft woven blanket, sat Ihsan. His pale, watery eyes alighted upon Zerdali and a smile crossed his deeply wrinkled, leathery face.

"*Günaydın*, Great-Grandfather," smiled Zerdali. "Good morning."

"*Günaydın*," replied Ihsan in a whispery voice. The edges of his lips curled upwards. "Every morning I see my Zerdali is a good morning," he added affectionately. He gazed down at the yellow plate on the tray that Zerdali rested on his frail knees. "What do we have here, my darling?"

Zerdali laughed. For as long as she could remember, Ihsan had been eating exactly the same breakfast – but he still managed to look surprised and delighted each morning.

"You have some *yagli sele*, the cured olives you love. There are some dried apricots. And you have an egg. Don't put too much salt on it, Great-Grandfather."

Ihsan felt the egg with a crooked brown finger.

"Ah," he said. "Just the way I like it."

"It has to be three minutes, Great-Grandfather," smiled Zerdali.

"Yes, it does," nodded Ihsan. "Three minutes each morning." He smiled, with a distant look in his eye.

As the sun rose into the azure-blue Turkish sky, the still air in the courtyard grew warmer and warmer. Ihsan fell asleep and dreamed of days gone by, tiny flecks of golden yolk drying in the whiskers beneath his lips. Zerdali crept out into the courtyard. She gently brushed the egg from her great-grandfather's face and cleared away the plate and the tray.

"He never eats the apricots," she said to Bahar, pointing at the deep-orange pieces of dried fruit, still neatly arranged on the plate where her mother had placed them earlier.

"No," said Bahar. "But if they're not there, he always asks for them."

Later that morning, there was a knock on the door of the house where Bahar, Zerdali and Ihsan lived.

Bahar, who was upstairs, lent out the window to see who was there.

"Baris!" she said, when she saw her brother kicking stones in the dusty street outside. She hurried downstairs. "*Nasılsınız*? How are you?"

"I will be a lot better with a glass of sweet apple tea," grinned Baris. "It's hot."

Bahar made apple tea while Baris and Zerdali chatted in the coolness of the kitchen.

"How's the backgammon?" asked Zerdali, teasing her uncle. Together with his friends, Baris spent hours in the local cafe, losing at backgammon and drinking tea.

"Ah," shrugged Baris. "As long as you lose with honour, you have not really lost."

"So, what brings you here today?" said Bahar, placing three tiny engraved glasses brimming with steaming apple tea on the table.

"Ihsan," replied Baris. "Old Ekrem, who owns the cafe, was asking if we wanted to do anything special for his birthday next week."

Bahar nodded. "At the cafe? That's a good idea. Our grandfather doesn't get out much these days."

"It's not too far to walk," said Baris. "And a lot of my friends there would like to see the old man again."

"He might even like to beat you at backgammon," grinned Zerdali cheekily.

Baris dropped a cube of sugar into his glass and stirred his tea vigorously. "I think, young lady, that he probably would," he replied with a wry smile.

2 A Story Never Told

Soon, Ihsan's ninety-seventh birthday arrived. In the morning, between games ofbackgammon, Old Ekrem and Baris had busied themselves, decorating the cafe with streamers and painting a sign that read: "*Doğum günün kutlu olsun*!" – "Happy Birthday!"

Many of the older men had dressed in faded old suits for the occasion, and some had even shaved.

Ihsan had taken some persuading to leave his courtyard. "I don't want any fuss," he declared. "It's just another day." But his grandchildren and his great-granddaughter persevered. Finally, he agreed to come to the celebration.

Despite his age and his weary bones, Ihsan was determined to walk. With short, hesitant steps, he headed towards the cafe, supported by Bahar and Zerdali on either side. And when he finally stepped through the doorway, he was greeted by a tremendous cheer and loud clapping.

"You know you are old when people cheer because you can walk," he whispered to Zerdali.

Zerdali and Bahar helped Ihsan into a chair. The town's mayor, Diyanat, was one of the men who had found a suit and a razor that morning. He strode to the small microphone that Ekrem had set up at the front of the cafe.

"Don't worry," he announced, "Diyanat will not be singing for you." There were murmurs of approval from the crowd. "Instead, I bring best wishes from all of our townsfolk, and I wish our friend Ihsan all the best on this special day."

For the next half hour, a parade of well-wishers took their place behind the microphone, and each shared a story about Ihsan.

Meanwhile, Old Ekrem carried swinging trays of apple tea to all the guests and made sure that the bowls of sweet, chewy *loki* on each table were kept replenished.

"I think he's enjoying this," Zerdali said to her mother, nodding in Ihsan's direction. His eyes were sparkling and he smiled as each person told a funny story about the old man.

Finally, when all the stories were told and everyone was settling in for a long afternoon's celebrations, Old Ekrem wiped his hands on a towel. He looked over at Ihsan and walked to the microphone. Everyone looked at him, waiting for another funny story.

"There is one story that has not yet been told," he said quietly, in his old, rasping voice. "Years ago, when Ihsan's father used to while away his retirement days in this cafe, he told me a tale which none of you have ever heard."

Everyone looked at Ihsan and then turned expectantly towards Old Ekrem.

"Ihsan's father was much better at backgammon than his poor grandson, Baris," chuckled the cafe owner ruefully. "And one day, long ago, we played. I promised not to repeat the story if I lost."

Zerdali frowned and looked at her great-grandfather. Ihsan shrugged. What was the story?

"I ask for forgiveness for breaking my promise," continued Old Ekrem solemnly. "But it is time that you should all know this story. I know you will never hear it from anyone else – least of all from Ihsan's lips."

The cafe fell silent. The people gathered at the tables looked at each other. This sounded serious. And then they listened, as Old Ekrem began the story that he had promised never to tell.

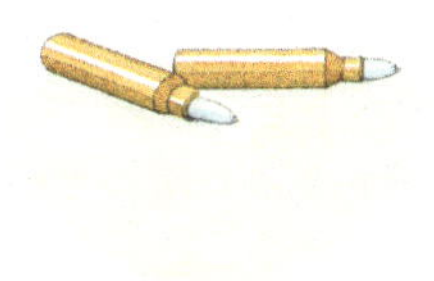

3 A Young Goatherd

Young Ihsan picked his way despondently through the deserted village of Krithia, anxiously looking this way and that. He felt sick. He knew what his father would say when he learnt that the goats Ihsan was supposed to have been watching had disappeared.

"*Sen nereye*?" Ihsan called in a worried voice. "Where are you?"

Ihsan had pleaded with his father for days to let him look after the goats.

"You are too young," his father had told him. "Goats have strong minds." But Ihsan had persisted and his father had finally given in.

The night before Ihsan's first day as a goatherd, the young boy had been excited – too excited to sleep. He quietly slipped out of bed well before dawn and, with a long stick and a low voice, coaxed the sleepy

goats along the stony path to their grazing ground. The goats, weary from their early start, had formed themselves into a ring and waited for the sun to rise.

In the strange half-light before dawn, Ihsan had climbed to a ledge above the deserted rocky hillside.

"Here is a good spot for a goatherd," he had declared, resting upon the ledge. Here, he would be able to watch wherever the goats grazed.

But, as the sun had finally broken above the horizon, and the warmth of the new spring day had slowly enveloped Ihsan, his sleepless night and early start had caught up with him. The new morning had found Ihsan, fast asleep, on his rocky ledge.

Time passed. After about an hour, the young boy woke up, his face feeling red and tight from the sun's rays. Strange noises, like the snapping of distant twigs, had disturbed his morning slumber. He sat bolt upright and anxiously scanned the grazing field below.

"Oh, no," he gasped.

With a feeling of panic, he realised the goats were nowhere to be seen.

Ihsan scrambled to his feet and clambered down the hillside, loose rocks slipping and clattering under his feet.

"*Sen nereye? Sen nereye?*" he called anxiously. "Where are you?"

The goats had vanished. Suddenly, Ihsan was distracted by a low, rumbling sound, which rolled its way over the hills to the west. There, a few kilometres beyond, lay the glistening Aegean Sea.

Ihsan put the rumbling out of his mind. He had to find the goats or he would be in big trouble. But where were they?

The young boy decided to search the overgrown pathway heading towards Krithia, knowing that the goats loved to fossick in the abandoned gardens for thistles and wild berries. He ran along the dusty path, praying that his hunch was correct.

Another deep, resounding rumble welled up from the west. Ihsan glanced up at the sky. No sign of thunderclouds. Then he had a thought. Here, on the outskirts of Krithia, he was close to the coastline. He knew the vibrations from the propellers of ships steaming their way through the narrow straits to the east could often be heard many kilometres inland. This must be the same noise – only coming from the sea to the west.

"That must be it," he reassured himself. He imagined the size of the giant ship that must be moving through the sea. Then he remembered the goats and he kept running. Finally, he arrived in the tiny square of the deserted village.

Hope soon turned to despair. Ihsan's heart plunged when he peered over the crumbling walls and into deserted gardens. The goats were nowhere to be seen.

With a rising feeling of dismay, he decided to keep searching westwards. He couldn't head home. His father, who had been reluctant to leave Ihsan alone with the goats, would be furious with him for falling asleep.

Old Ekrem stopped recounting his tale and took a sip of steaming apple tea. Everyone in the cafe was transfixed by Old Ekrem's storytelling. He gazed out at his audience, all of whom were waiting to hear what happened next. But he avoided the pale eyes of Ihsan, who he knew would not be so keen to hear the next chapter.

But, thought Old Ekrem, I have started. Now there is no going back. He cleared his throat and continued.

4 A Ferocious Storm

Between the dusty wasteland where the village ruins petered out and the tall Turkish pines mustered themselves into a thick forest, there grew a single wild apricot tree.

Even in the old days, when families had called Krithia home, the tree had been ancient. Young Ihsan stopped for a moment and took a deep breath. The smell of wild apricot blossom filled his lungs. He noticed three mottled and bruised apricots from last year's crop, scattered on the ground beneath the branches. He filled his pockets. In his excitement to leave the house before dawn, he'd forgotten to take a chunk of bread for his breakfast. The sight of the wild apricots suddenly reminded him that he was starving.

Ihsan, desperate to find his troublesome goats, headed into the Turkish pines. Out of the sun, it was cooler and darker. But the shade also cooled his spirits. The breeze rustling the pine branches seemed disturbed and slightly sinister. All the time, the unnerving rumbling was growing louder, not more distant. The cracks and snaps that pierced the air were getting sharper and closer. The shadows of the forest and the unexplained noises added to Ihsan's growing feelings of unease.

"*Sen nereye?*" he called nervously. Something was wrong. Ihsan was overwhelmed by the voice in his head, urging him to find his goats and head home as soon as he could. The forest was not welcoming the young boy. It was warning him.

Fighting the feeling of fear rising from his stomach, Ihsan pressed on, deeper and deeper into the forest.

"I must find my goats," he said to himself, ignoring the warnings that every sense in his body was sending him.

Suddenly, the forest opened up into a small clearing. Sunlight dappled through the lofty pines. Ihsan took a step, about to enter the clearing, then stopped, petrified. The sunlight dancing on the trees made it seem to Ihsan that the whole clearing was trembling.

Then, through the trees, he caught sight of mysterious dark shadows moving stealthily, flicking in and out of sight between the gnarly trunks.

He was not alone.

The cafe was silent. At every table, apple tea cooled, the glasses untouched. The bowls of *loki* remained full. No one moved. The only sound was the low hum of the ceiling fan, lazily swirling the hot Turkish air around the room.

A birthday streamer fluttered in the breeze from the fan. But everyone's concentration was firmly focused on Old Ekrem. He paused for a second then took up the story again.

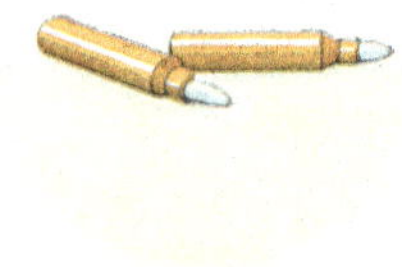

Terrified, Ihsan dropped to the ground. He pressed his body into the thick layer of pine needles that carpeted the damp earth. Then the shadows became men.

A strange shout echoed through the trees. His face pressed into the pine needles, Ihsan heard the scuffing of boots as the shadows moved closer. He prayed that he would not be seen. Then someone said something in a language that Ihsan had never heard before.

The young boy's mind whirled. He raised his head a fraction. What was happening? Who were these strangers?

Then, without warning, a lone horse rider galloped through the Turkish pines. Instantly, the terrifying clouds of suspense that filled the clearing exploded into a deadly storm.

A volley of deafening shots split the air. Horrified, Ihsan saw the horse rider slump in his saddle and struggle to wheel his horse around. Someone shouted. Another volley of shots burst through the trees. And, from the direction of Krithia, Ihsan heard the sound of more hooves racing towards the forest, like heavy raindrops thundering upon a roof.

Stunned by what was unfolding in the forest, Ihsan saw a dozen horse riders streaming through the clearing at full gallop.

"Soldiers," gasped Ihsan, recognising the dull grey uniform of the Ottoman Army. At the head of the horse riders, bent double and urging his steed on, was an officer, sword drawn, shouting ferociously.

In an instant, the whole forest erupted into another deafening storm of gunfire. A heavy smell filled the clearing and stung Ihsan's eyes. The officer shouted to his men, and the soldiers leapt from their horses and scrambled for cover.

Ihsan found himself shaking uncontrollably. Pressing himself desperately against the trunk of a Turkish pine, he wished that the tree would open up and swallow him. The air around Ihsan sounded like it was filled with a swarm of angry, buzzing hornets. He closed his eyes in terror. He knew these were not insects. These were *bullets.*

Suddenly, Ihsan heard a thumping sound. He opened his eyes. One of the strange shadows, bent low, was sprinting straight towards him.

A split-second later, the air was torn apart with the sound of another furious hornet, speeding towards its target.

Ihsan waited for the sting.

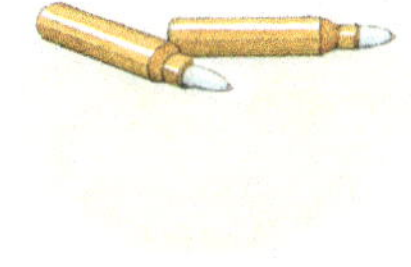

5 Two Frightened Boys

The shadow crashed into the ground with a sickening thud. Ihsan pressed himself hard into the tree trunk, daring not to breathe.

With a horrified glance at the shadow sprawled in front of him, Ihsan realised that this man was a soldier, too. But he was not an Ottoman soldier. He wore a felt hat, with one side pinned to the brim. And his uniform was a muddy brown khaki – except for the left shoulder, where a spreading patch of deep, dark red stained his tunic.

With a groan, the soldier rolled onto his side. And then, with a shock, their frightened eyes met.

Ihsan gasped. He'd always imagined soldiers to be grim, fierce men, hardened by endless battles. But this soldier was not much older than Ihsan. And he looked scared.

The soldier whispered something in the strange language. Then he grimaced, wracked with pain. Ihsan saw the red stain seeping down the young soldier's tunic.

It was as if Ihsan's world had suddenly shrunk. There was only him, a wounded soldier, and an arm's length of pine needles between them. The whizzing of the hornets and the deafening cracks of the rifles faded into the background. For a second, nothing else mattered.

Ihsan's mind raced. He had seen his father help another villager who had been attacked by a bull. He knew straightaway that he had to stop the bleeding. He forced himself away from the safety of the tree trunk and crawled to where the soldier lay. The young man's eyes gazed at him and he gasped something else.

Ihsan shook his head. "I don't understand," he replied. He pulled open the young man's tunic and, without a moment's hesitation, pressed his small palm onto the wound in the man's bloodied shoulder.

The soldier winced and screwed up his face in pain.

"I'm sorry," said Ihsan. He pressed as hard as he could, trying to stem the flow of the sticky blood. He looked up, hoping that somehow this madness would cease and that someone would come to his assistance. But the soldiers on either side of the clearing had regrouped behind clumps of Turkish pines and the air was still thick with red-hot hornets.

The fallen soldier said something again. Ihsan looked at him, and the young man pointed to a small khaki flask strapped to his knee. Reaching down, Ihsan pulled the flask free and poured a few drops of water into the soldier's mouth.

The soldier nodded at Ihsan and smiled. Ihsan realised his own mouth was dry with fear and took a sip of the water. Then he splashed some over the soldier's wound.

Ihsan needed to find a bandage. For once, he was grateful to his mother for insisting he always carry a handkerchief. He plunged his free hand into his pocket. But instead of linen, his fingers felt the smooth outline of three wild apricots, the ones he had collected from Krithia.

He pulled one out and offered it to the wounded soldier. He watched as the young man closed his eyes and breathed deeply, filling his nostrils with the scent of the apricot. Then his eyes flickered open again and he smiled. Ihsan twisted the apricot in two and placed one half in the young man's mouth.

Ihsan's world closed in again. For a minute, there was nothing but two boys, sharing an apricot.

Little did young Ihsan know that, throughout his long, long life, he would remember that unreal moment each and every day. The absurdity of two strangers enjoying wild apricots beneath a sky filled with a storm of deadly bullets.

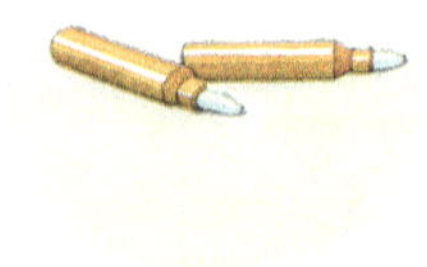

Zerdali wiped a tear away from the corner of her eye. She glanced over at her mother, Bahar. They both looked at each other with the same dawning realisation. The three apricots. Neatly arranged, each morning. Ihsan never ate them. He just enjoyed their sweet aroma and the memories that they stirred within him.

Young Ihsan found his handkerchief and pressed it onto the hurt soldier's shoulder. In his compressed world, minutes seemed like hours. But despite his best efforts, Ihsan couldn't stop the blood from seeping out of the wound. The young man was growing weaker and weaker, and his eyes began to grow dull.

Ihsan knew he had to summon up all of his courage. Right now.

He carefully prised the warm, wet handkerchief off the young man's shoulder and, scrabbling around among the pine needles, his hand closed over a small branch that had fallen near the tree. His fingers trembled as he tied one corner of the linen to the top of the branch.

Then, shaking with fear, he slowly raised his bloodied flag. Young Ihsan got to his feet.

6 Three Fingers

Surprised men shouted from the edges of the clearing, and the hornets died away. The fury of the battle was replaced by a terrible, eerie silence. Ihsan's feet felt like they were made of heavy lead, but he forced himself to take a step into the clearing.

The fighting soldiers, shocked by what they saw, watched the boy take another step in the direction of the foreign soldiers. Every nerve in Ihsan's body was screaming. But he took another step. And another.

As he approached, Ihsan could make out the grim faces of the foreign soldiers beneath their hats. Their steely eyes watched him suspiciously as he drew closer. He stopped and pointed to the bloody flag. Then he pointed to the tree trunk where he and the wounded soldier had been sheltering from the blaze of bullets.

Two of the foreign soldiers whispered something urgently to each other. One shook his head. The other nodded emphatically and said something to Ihsan. Ihsan looked at him blankly.

Then, incredibly, the foreign soldier who had spoken put down his rifle and cautiously raised

his hands. A look of determination flashed across his face and he stepped out from his position into the clearing.

There was a shout from the Ottoman soldiers and an instant barking order from their officer.

The hornets remained silent.

With hands raised, the foreign soldier carefully walked towards Ihsan. With aching slowness, together they inched their way towards the wounded soldier, as the others watched their every movement.

The foreign soldier slowly dropped his hands. He knelt down and heaved his wounded comrade into a sitting position. The young soldier was weak, but his eyes flickered open, and he smiled at Ihsan. The foreign soldier linked his arms around the wounded man's chest while Ihsan lifted the man's feet clear of the pine needles. Together, they carried the wounded soldier back towards his comrades.

When they reached the group of foreign soldiers, two other comrades dragged the wounded young man into the trees beyond the clearing. The foreign soldiers who remained at the clearing's edge nodded at Ihsan. Their eyes flicked across the clearing. Suddenly, no one knew what to do. Ihsan stood exposed, helpless, with no idea of what would happen next.

The foreign soldier who had carried the wounded soldier across the clearing stepped back out of cover. He turned to where the Ottoman soldiers were crouching and called out to them in a strong voice. The air was electric with danger.

The soldier tapped his wristwatch, pointed at Ihsan and held up three fingers. Then he waved urgently at Ihsan, pointing towards the forest beyond the clearing. He held up three fingers again.

Ihsan, terrified that the shooting would start again any second, took to his heels and ran as fast as he could. It was only years later that he realised what the three fingers meant.

"Three minutes. Give the boy three minutes."

"And that is the end of my story," said Old Ekrem. He looked across at the silent faces, all of whom had turned to watch Ihsan. The old man looked tired and his eyes flicked from face to face.

"I'm sorry, Ihsan," said Old Ekrem. "I have broken my promise. But only because your family deserves to know what the name 'Ihsan' really means."

Zerdali, Baris and Bahar were astounded. As Old Ekrem had rightly guessed, they'd never heard the story from Ihsan.

"It means 'compassion'," finished Old Ekrem. "But since that morning, it really means 'hero'."

For a full minute, no one moved. There was not a word spoken. There was no noise, except the dull whirr of the cafe fan.

Then Diyanat, the mayor, stood up and walked over to Ihsan. He shook the frail old man's hand. He whispered something into Baris's ear.

Ihsan slowly shook away the memories that he thought had been lost many years ago.

"Help me up, my dear," he said to Zerdali.

Zerdali helped her great-grandfather to his feet, and he slowly turned to face the people in the cafe.

He stood for a moment, and everyone waited to hear what he would say.

The old man smiled. "I still got into trouble for losing my goats," he said.

7 Time to Remember

One month later, Zerdali and Bahar were preparing Ihsan's breakfast, as they always did. Some black olives. Three dried apricots. One egg, boiled for exactly three minutes. But this morning, there was something else.

An official-looking letter had arrived, addressed to Ihsan. Bahar popped it onto the tray, next to the yellow plate, and Zerdali headed out to where her great-grandfather was dozing, shaded by the old olive tree in the courtyard.

"*Günaydın*, Great-Grandfather," smiled Zerdali. "Good morning."

"*Günaydın*," replied Ihsan in his whispery voice. He gazed down at the yellow plate on the tray that Zerdani rested on his frail knees. He picked up the envelope and turned it suspiciously in his fingers. "What do we have here, my darling?"

"I don't know," she replied. "Open it and see."

Ihsan pulled open the flap of the envelope and drew out a thick piece of paper. He stared at it.

"My eyesight's not too good these days," he said to Zerdali. "You read it to me."

Zerdali took the letter and read its contents.

"It seems Diyanat has written to the provincial governor," she said, looking at Ihsan. "You have been asked to be the governor's guest of honour at next month's annual memorial at Anzac Cove."

Ihsan looked at his egg and prodded it gently with his finger. "Ah," he said. "Just the way I like it."

"Great-Grandfather," pressed Zerdali. "It's a great honour. You will attend, won't you?"

Ihsan smiled at his great-granddaughter and shook his head. "No, my dear, I will not go," he smiled. "Those hills, those forests, those memorials. It is too eerie a place for an old man."

"But ..." started Zerdali.

"The wind blows too many lost souls across those jagged hills and overgrown gullies. It is a place of memories that should not be disturbed."

Zerdali looked disappointed, but Ihsan found her hand and squeezed it gently.

"Don't be sad, my dear," he said. "It will not be many months before I meet my Anzac friends again. I've kept them waiting for a long time."

Zerdali opened her mouth to protest, but Ihsan smiled happily and held up his hand.

"Until then, I am surrounded by all that I need. I have peace, the spirit of youth and the sweet scent of wild apricots."

Zerdali looked puzzled. Ihsan's watery eyes twinkled conspiratorially.

"Those are your names, my dear. Did you not know?"

Zerdali shook her head.

"'Baris' means peace. 'Bahar' means the spirit of youth. 'Zerdali' means wild apricots," smiled Ihsan. "Each morning, my day begins with a reminder of that morning, and the good things that came to pass after those terrible times."

He prodded his egg again.

“Three minutes?” he said.

Zerdali smiled and held up three fingers.

“Three minutes,” she nodded. “Don’t worry, Great-Grandfather. We’ll always remember, at the start of every morning.”